China Tells How the World Began!

As told by Miwa Kurita

Edited by Miyoko Matsutani
Illustrated by Saoko Mitsukuri
Translated by Matthew Galgani

HEIAN

Hearing Tales as They Are Told

Do you love to listen to stories? I do. Can you listen really well?

For hundreds of years, people have passed down folktales from grandparents and parents to children by telling—not writing—them.

When people tell you a story, you don't just hear with your ears. You learn a lot from the voices the storytellers use, how they move their arms, legs, head, shoulders, and body, the expressions on their face—all the tools they use to make their tales come alive.

This book, and the others in the series Asian Folktales Retold, was created to help you truly "hear" Asian folktales and understand them deeply.

As you listen to these tales, or perhaps read them yourself when you're older, figure out for yourself what they mean. If you can hear the storyteller's voice in your head, then you are listening really well.

Published by HEIAN, P.O. Box 8208, Berkeley, California 94707
HEIAN is an imprint of Stone Bridge Press
www.stonebridge.com • sbp@stonebridge.com

© 2001 Miyoko Matsutani
Originally published in Japan by Hoshinowakai

LIBRARY OF CONGRESS CATALOGING-IN-PUBLICATION DATA
Kurita, Miwa, 1982–
  [Shojo ga hakonda Chugoku minwa Selections.]
  China tells how the world began! / as told by Miwa Kurita ; edited by Miyoko Matsutani ; illustrated by Saoko Mitsukuri.
    p. cm. — (Asian folktales retold)
  Originally published in Japan by Hoshinowakai, ©2001 under the title, Shojo ga hakonda Chugoku minwa in the series, Ajia kokoro no minwa.
  Summary: Two Chinese folktales, one about how the ancient god created heaven and earth with his body, and the other explaining how the years were named after animals.
  ISBN-13: 978-0-89346-944-3
  ISBN-10: 0-89346-944-0
  [1. Folklore—China.] I. Matsutani, Miyoko, 1926– II. Mitsukuri, Saoko, 1970– ill. III. Title. IV. Series.
  PZ8.1.K982Chi   2006
  398.20951'01—dc22

                                        2005035630

How the World Began

A long, long time ago, the universe was nothing more than a soupy mush—can you imagine? Then an egg shape appeared. What do you think was inside?

It was an ancient god, sleeping.

Well, millions of years passed by. Then, one day, the god woke up, at last. Everything was pitch black and slimy! Of course, this made the god feel awfully uncomfortable.

The god stretched out his arms, to break the egg's shell, and stepped outside. The slimy goo inside the egg flowed out into the nothingness, and guess what? It became the seven continents of our world.

The delicate eggshell floated up and became the heavens. But the heavens were so light, they looked as if they would soon drift down to earth again.

So, to keep the heavens from falling, the ancient god held them up with his head. And to stop the egg's slimy goo from flowing any farther, he held the continents down with his feet.

As time went on, the
heavens slowly inched higher,
and the earth's continents
became harder.

All this time the ancient
god was holding the earth down
with his feet and holding the
heavens up with his head. But
he mysteriously grew bigger
day by day.

Now, thousands of years
passed.

Then, the ancient god let
go of the heavens. What do you
think happened?

The heavens did *not* come drifting down to earth again!

When the ancient god saw this, he felt in a sudden rush how tired he had been for thousands of years. First he sat down heavily, and then he lay down, turning onto his side.

"Aaah," he breathed, giving a deep, deep sigh of relief. And then he died.

His great sigh became the wind that still blows today. His hair—blown upward by the wind—touched the heavens and became the stars in the sky.

His left eye became the sun. His right eye became the moon.

And, in time, the blood flowed from his body and became the oceans.

The god's veins became the mountains and the rivers. His skin became the fields and the prairies. His sweat became the rain and the dew that forms at night.

So, now you know: with his body, the ancient god created heaven and earth.

And that is how the world began.

Why Cats Hate Rats

Once upon a time, people had no way of remembering what year it was.

They decided one day to ask the gods to help them.

"Please give us an easy way to remember each year," they said.

The gods thought and thought. Finally, they answered. "How about this idea: we could choose twelve kinds of animals and use one as a symbol for each year. Animals are easy to remember."

"That's a great idea!" the people said. "We'll count every twelve years and then start over again."

But there was one problem: which animals should they use as symbols?

The gods decided to have all the animals race across the river. Then the first twelve animals to finish the race would be the symbols for the twelve years, in the order they crossed the finish line.

Which animals do you think are going to finish first? You might be surprised.

To tell all the animals about the race, the gods made a big sign.

First it told the animals about naming the twelve years. Then it said: "So, we are going to have a race across the river. If you want to have *one* of the twelve years named for you and you alone, please come to the race."

Of course, the animals were all
buzzing, barking, squealing, and squeaking
with excitement.

"I know I'm going to be one of the twelve,"
each animal said to itself. "No, not just *one* of the
twelve, the very first!"

Now, in those days, the cat and the rat were the best of friends. Is that hard to believe? It's true. But there was one problem: neither one could swim. How could they cross the river and win the race?

The cat had an idea: "Let's go find the ox. I'm sure he'll help us race across the river." So that's what they did.

At last, the day of the big race came.

While it was still dark, the cat and the rat woke the ox. He let them both climb on his back, and he waded into the river.

"We're almost across now. We're going to be first!" the cat shouted with glee. "Go, go, Mr. Ox!"

20

Just then, the rat rammed into the cat with all his might and
sent her tumbling into the river with a splash. He watched her fall,
feeling quite proud of himself. Then, he chomped his sharp teeth into
the ox's tail.

"Ow, ow, ow!" squealed the ox in great pain. He flipped his tail up
into the air, flinging the rat across to the other side of the river.

The rat landed smack at the feet of the gods waiting at the
finish line.

"So *you're* the first to finish!" said the gods in great surprise.

"If you please, gods," said the rat, "I may be small, but I'm smart."

The ox then came crawling up the bank of the river, shouting. "Yes, yes! I did it! I'm the winner! I'm number one!"

"Actually, no," said the gods. "You came in second. The rat got here before you."

The ox couldn't believe it. He opened his eyes as wide as he could and looked back at his tail, expecting to see the rat still there. He had no idea what had happened.

Next, along came the tiger, calling "I'm number one! I'm number one!"

The gods just laughed and held up three fingers.

With an angry scowl, the
tiger was about to protest when
everything around him turned
dark. Looking up, the tiger saw the
dragon coming down from the sky,
riding on a cloud.

23

Just as the gods were about to raise four fingers, down at their feet they heard a voice saying "The rabbit's already here."

The gods looked down to see a small rabbit sitting politely. "Oh," they said. "Well, then, the rabbit is number four."

And that is how the dragon took fifth place.

After a little while, the horse appeared, giving a neigh of delight.

"Here's number six!" said the gods.

But just before the horse could reach the finish line, the snake slithered up and hissed loudly, "The sssnake is sssixth. Sssssee? I ssslid in firssst."

Close behind the horse came the sheep, the monkey, and the rooster.

What numbers did they win?

Now most of the places were taken.

The dog came paddling in next, taking the number eleven place. He would have arrived a lot sooner if he hadn't been dillydallying.

"Who," asked the gods, "is going to win the final spot?"

Nir

Ten

Eleven

Five

Eight

Seven

Four

Six

Three

Two

One

Just then, the pig came dashing in, panting heavily.

"Does anyone, oink, have something good, oink, to eat? I got up extra early this morning, oink, and I'm extra starving."

The first twelve animals had now arrived. So, the gods declared, "We will now announce the twelve winners in order: the rat, the ox, the tiger, the rabbit . . ."

But before they could go any further, the soaking wet cat came running up to the finish line. "What number am I?" she asked, dripping.

"Sorry, you're a little too late," the gods answered kindly. "The race is over."

The fur on the back of the cat's neck rose stiffly, and, with an angry yowl, she sprang at the rat. The rat ran to hide behind the gods.

So, from that day on, whenever a cat sees a rat, she attacks him in a flash.

The rat may have taken first place in the race to name the years, but every day he must live in fear of the cat, always looking over his shoulder.

About the Series and This Book

The Asian Folktales Retold series was created to capture the spirit of Asian folktales and give them new life, showing children how these stories help us both evaluate the modern world and connect with a rich cultural past. The stories strive to preserve the oral flavor of recountings of tales passed down for generations, and they are intended to be read aloud to experience the full joy of this picture book.

The Chinese folktales in this book were told by Miwa Kurita to folktale researcher Keiko Nomura, who was seeking a glimpse into "the Chinese soul." Nomura found that the stories transcended borders and nationalities, and she was motivated to publish them to open a window into the heart of Asia for everyone. Through exchanges of folktales that reveal the essence of a culture, people from different backgrounds can develop understanding and friendship across international boundaries.

About the Storyteller

Miwa Kurita, whose Chinese name is Chisa Fue, was born in Jilin, China, in 1982. She moved to Japan in 1998 when her Chinese mother, Reiko, married her Japanese stepfather, Shotaro Kurita. Miwa brought many folktales with her as a reminder of her native land. She was beginning to learn Japanese when folktale researcher Keiko Nomura visited the Kurita family and asked Miwa to share her Chinese folktales.

About the Illustrator

Born in 1970 in Shinjuku, Tokyo, Saoko Mitsukuri graduated from Musashino Art University. After studying in Korea, she became familiar with the Philippines, China, Nepal, and other Asian cultures, traveling and sketching extensively. She has illustrated several publications.

To prepare for illustrating this book, Mitsukuri did extensive research in Jilin, Miwa Kurita's birthplace in China, meeting with Miwa's grandmother, aunts, and cousins. She strove to portray the essence of the Chinese folktales in her drawings.

About Jilin, the Storyteller's Birthplace

By Lee Chi, *Research Specialist, Yamagata University*

Located in China's northeast region, Jilin is home to approximately 1.4 million people. More than 80 percent of the city's population is of Han heritage; 10 percent is Korean, and the remainder a mix of Manchurian and several other ethnic groups. The people speak the Northern dialect of Mandarin—a close relative of the Beijing dialect.

The Songhua River runs through the city like an S, and you can sometimes spot a fishing boat or freighter floating down it. China's leading scientific base is nearby.

Jilin is known as a producer of rice, corn, soybeans, fruit, and other crops. It has a timber industry and is a supplier of sable pelts.

At the upper reaches of the river is the electricity-generating Fengman Dam, built long ago by the Japanese. In the city's constructed Songhua Lake you can catch countless varieties of fish.

Winters are quite cold, and Jilin is famous for the white frost that coats the winter landscape, drawing people from all over the world to see it. The surrounding area is a ski resort in winter, and the Winter Asian Games have been held there several times.

Acknowledgments

Folktale researcher Kazuo Yoshizawa offered me passionate and dedicated assistance in pursuing these folktales and introduced me to Miyoko Matsutani, who became the executive consultant for the series.

Matsutani gave life to the book and supported it. Collaborating directly with storytellers, she has written numerous books that showcase folktales, capturing in print the depth and flow of the original oral tradition. Matsutani directs the Miyoko Matsutani Center for Folktale Research and is a member of the Japanese Folktale Association.

The Mamurogawa Folktale Club and storyteller Toshiko Shibata gave Miwa encouragement and support.

We also received assistance from Lee Chi, like Miwa from Jilin, China, who was studying at Yamagata University, and from Professor Tsuneo Ishijima of Yamagata University and Taizan Hasegawa of the Joetsu University of Education.

Tomio Togashi, who photographed the storyteller and the illustrator for this book, introduced me to Miwa Kurita.

I want to thank these and all the many people who made this book possible.

Keiko Nomura
Folktale Researcher
Executive Editor of Asian Folktales Retold